3 0132 02416272 4

NORTHUMBERLAND COUNTY LIBRARY

You should return this book on or before the last date stamped below unless an extension of the loan ~~~~~~~~~~ ted.

Application for rer ~~~~~~~~~~ phone.

D1139053

Fines at the appro ~~~~~~~~~~ ok is overdue.

BERWICK UPON TWEED

LIBRARY   10/14

2 2 NOV 2014   LYNEMOUTH 8/17

2 9 SEP 2015
1 8 AUG 2017   3/17

Short Sharp Shakespeare Stories

A Midsummer Nights Dream

Retold by Anna Claybourne

Illustrated by Tom Morgan-Jones

WAYLAND
www.waylandbooks.co.uk

First published in 2014 by Wayland

Copyright © Wayland 2014
Wayland
338 Euston Road
London NW1 3BH

Wayland Australia
Level 17/207 Kent Street
Sydney, NSW 2000

All rights reserved

Editor: Elizabeth Brent
Design: Amy McSimpson
Illustration: Tom Morgan-Jones

A catalogue for this title is available from the British Library
Dewey number: 823.9'2-dc23

10 9 8 7 6 5 4 3 2 1

ISBN: 978 0 7502 9110 1
eBook ISBN: 978 0 7502 8808 8
Library eBook ISBN: 978 0 7502 9351 8

Printed in China
Wayland is a division of Hachette Children's Books,
an Hachette UK company
www.hachette.co.uk

WAYLAND
www.waylandbooks.co.uk

CONTENTS

INTRODUCING
A MIDSUMMER NIGHT'S DREA

A Midsummer Night's Dream is one of Shakespeare's best-loved plays. He wrote several types of play, ranging from gory, horror-filled tragedies to the lightest and silliest of comedies.

In Shakespeare's time, a "comedy" didn't just mean something funny, like a modern sitcom. It meant a light-hearted story with a happy ending. However, Shakespeare's comedies were often very funny too, and *A Midsummer Night's Dream* is one of the funniest.

Who was Shakespeare?

William Shakespeare is known today as a great writer - one of the greatest of all time. He lived around 400 years ago, working mainly in London as a playwright and actor for a theatre company. These days, Shakespeare's language sounds old-fashioned, but his works are still widely performed and very popular.

What's the story?

Theseus, Duke of Athens, is about to marry Hippolyta, and the local workmen are preparing a play to perform at the wedding. But for four young lovers, true love is not running quite so smoothly. When the fairies try to use magic to sort things out, a series of mindboggling mix-ups results. Read on to begin the romantic, yet ridiculous story of *A Midsummer Night's Dream...*

A Midsummer Night's Dream: Who's who?

Every Shakespeare play starts with a list of characters, called the *dramatis personae*.

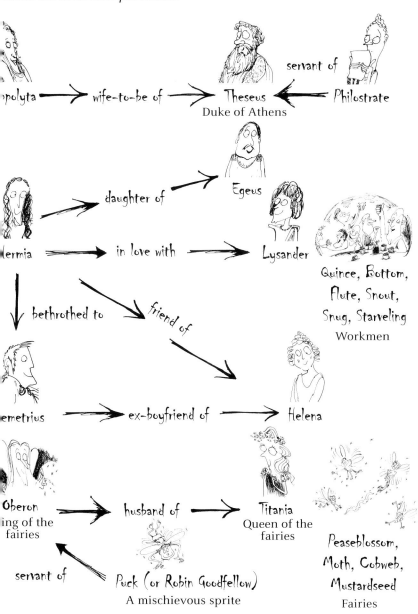

Hippolyta → wife-to-be of → Theseus
Duke of Athens

servant of ← Philostrate

Hermia → daughter of → Egeus

Hermia → in love with → Lysander

Quince, Bottom,
Flute, Snout,
Snug, Starveling
Workmen

Hermia → bethrothed to → Demetrius

friend of →

Demetrius → ex-boyfriend of → Helena

Oberon
King of the fairies → husband of → Titania
Queen of the fairies

Puck (or Robin Goodfellow)
A mischievous sprite

servant of → Oberon

Peaseblossom,
Moth, Cobweb,
Mustardseed
Fairies

Chapter One

Theseus, the Duke of Athens, could not believe his luck. In just a few days, he would marry Hippolyta. The queen of the Amazon warrior tribe, she was tall, bold, brave and beautiful. They had met as enemies, but had instantly fallen in love.

"Just four more days until May Day, my darling," he smiled, "and then we'll be married."

Hippolyta kissed him. "And those four days will pass in the blink of an eye, like magic!" she said.

"Philostrate," Theseus called, "is everything ready for the wedding?"

"Yes, sir!" His chief servant appeared. "There'll be a five-course wedding feast, and a big party for everyone in Athens! It's going to be wonderful!"

"And what about some entertainment – like some music, or something?" asked Theseus. "Philostrate, go and ask the people of Athens to come up with something. They can all offer their talents, and on our wedding night, we'll choose the best!"

"An excellent idea, my Lord!" Philostrate cried, clapping his hands.

Four days will quickly **steep** themselves in night.
Four days will quickly **dream** away the time.

What does that mean!?
"Steep" means soak. Hippolyta says
the days will become nights as if they
are being plunged into dark liquid.

As Philostrate left, Egeus, a nobleman of Athens, came up to Theseus. With him were his beautiful daughter, Hermia, and two young men.

"Theseus, you must help me!" Egeus exclaimed. "I don't know what to do with this disobedient daughter of mine!" Hermia stood scowling at his side, with her raven-dark ringlets and flashing eyes.

"Do go on, Egeus," Theseus said.

"Well, I've chosen a husband for her – this fine, young man, Demetrius." Egeus pointed to one of the men – a tall, blond and handsome youth.

"He's keen to marry her too, of course. But THIS man, Lysander, has been wooing her – turning her head with love poems and soppy songs – and now she says she loves him instead!" He pointed to the dreamy-eyed, dark-haired Lysander.

Theseus turned to Hermia. "Hermia, the law of Athens says you must marry the man your father chooses. And Demetrius does seem like a nice man."

"Not as nice as Lysander," Hermia snorted.

"But Demetrius is your father's choice," said Theseus.

"Well, he's not my choice," said Hermia,

"so I'm **not** marrying him. I refuse. So there."

"OK," said Theseus, "according to the law, if you refuse, you must either be put to death, or become a nun and never see another man again. A silly law, I admit, but there it is."

"Fine," said Hermia. "I'll be a nun. I don't want to see any other men, if I can't have Lysander!"

"Hot-headed Hermia, don't rush into things," said Theseus kindly. "Take some time to think about it. I'll give you until May Day, my wedding day, to decide."

At this point, Demetrius butted in. "Please, Hermia, just marry me, and forget this fool."

"Fool yourself," retorted Lysander. "If her father loves you so much, why don't you just marry him?"
Egeus's mouth fell open in outrage.

"Hermia and I are in love," Lysander told Theseus.
"But Demetrius can't even decide who he loves!
Not long ago, he was wooing Helena, and wanted
to marry her, and she's still in love with him!"

What does that mean!?
"Do you marry him" is not
a question, but means
"Go on, you marry him!"

"That's enough," Theseus said. "Egeus, Demetrius, come with me, and we'll talk about this."

The truth was, Theseus felt sorry for Hermia. Why couldn't she marry the man she loved, just as he could marry Hippolyta? He hoped he could persuade Egeus and Demetrius to change their minds.

When they were gone, Hermia began to sob. Lysander hugged her. "Don't worry, my love," he whispered. "In books, true love always meets with terrible obstacles. Our problems simply prove that our love is real."

The course of true love never did run smooth.

"And that we must be patient, and find a way around them," Hermia added.

"Exactly! And guess what – I've got a brilliant idea. The law of Athens says you can't marry me – so let's run away and get married somewhere else! I have a rich aunt in the next town who I'm sure will help us. Sneak out of your house tomorrow night, and meet me in the forest outside the city walls."

"Oh, Lysander!" Hermia cried. "Of course! Now we can be together forever!"

Just then, Helena came along. She and Hermia were old friends, but she was very jealous that Demetrius wanted to marry Hermia instead of her. She still loved him.

"Helena!" said Hermia. "How are you?"

"I feel terrible, if you must know," said Helena bitterly. "And I look terrible too, compared to you. Oh, if only I had your beauty, Hermia, Demetrius might love me!"

Helena was not ugly – she was very pretty, with fair hair, rosy cheeks and a sweet smile. But all she could think about was that Demetrius didn't like her.

"Don't worry, Helena," Hermia said. "I'm not marrying Demetrius."

"It's true," said Lysander. "We're going to run away together into the forest, tomorrow night. But please don't tell anyone."

Helena promised not to tell a soul. But as soon as Hermia and Lysander had gone, she decided she might tell just one person – Demetrius. Perhaps it would make him like her more. And if that didn't work, at least it would give her a chance to talk to him...

She hurried off to find Demetrius at once.

Hermia and Lysander weren't the only Athenians making a plan. In a higgledy-piggledy house near the duke's palace, Quince the carpenter had gathered his friends together. There was Bottom the weaver, Snug the joiner, Snout the tinker, Starveling the tailor, and Flute the bellows-maker.

Quince had always wanted to star in a play, and now was his chance! That very morning, he had heard that the Duke wanted the people of Athens – simple workmen like himself – to provide the entertainment at his wedding feast.

Quince had chosen a play, and he had enough friends for all the parts. All they had to do was practise it a few times, and they would be ready!

"Now then," he called. "Are we all here?"

"We are!" said Bottom. "So what play are we putting on, Quince?"

"Ahem," said Quince, unrolling a battered old script. "The play is called *The Most Lamentable Comedy and Most Cruel Death of Pyramus and Thisbe.*"

"It sounds great!" said Bottom.
"What's my part?"

"I've got you down for Pyramus," said Quince, "a star-crossed lover who dies for love."

"Oh, I'll be fantastic!" declared Bottom. "I'll have the whole audience in tears!"

"You, Flute," Quince went on, "will play Thisbe, his lady love."

"Oh no, please, not the girl's part!" moaned Flute. "I'm growing a beard!"

Quince ignored him. "Snout, you're Pyramus's father; Starveling, Thisbe's mother; and I will play Thisbe's father. And Snug – you're the lion."

Nay, faith, let me not play a woman. I have a beard coming.

What does that mean!?
"Faith" used in this way is like saying "I swear" or "really!"

"But I'm useless at learning lines," Snug complained. "Do we have to do this?"

"You'll be fine," said Quince. "I've given you the easiest part – it's just roaring."

"I could do that too!" interrupted Bottom.

"No, you have to be Pyramus," Quince said. "Now, we don't want anyone overhearing what we're planning, or even worse, copying our play. So we won't rehearse in Athens – we'll meet in the forest tomorrow night and rehearse there instead."

Chapter Two

The forest outside Athens was a strange, enchanted place. As dusk fell, fairies and sprites flitted through its flowery glades, unseen by human eyes.

In fact, Oberon and Titania, the fairy king and queen, were in the forest that very night. They had come to Athens to give Theseus's wedding their magical blessing. But Oberon and Titania themselves were not getting on at all. They were furious with each other.

It's a well-known fact that fairies sometimes steal away the prettiest, most perfect human babies to keep for themselves. And Titania had a new human child all of her own. He was a little Indian prince, the son of a king. His mother had died, and Titania had taken him to be her pageboy.

Oberon was horribly jealous. As soon as he saw the beautiful child, he wanted him for himself – but Titania refused.

Now, they were avoiding each other. But as Titania made her way through the trees, followed by her fairy servants, she bumped right into Oberon and his servant sprite, Puck.

"Oh," she scowled. "It's you."

"Nice to see you, Titania," said Oberon. *"NOT."*

"Come on, fairies," the queen snapped. "Let's go somewhere else. I'm not speaking to him."

"Titania, just give me that boy and we'll be friends. You should do what I say – I'm your husband, after all."

"Oh, are you!?" Titania sneered. "Well, in that case, you should only have eyes for me. But I know who you really fancy – that big battleaxe Hippolyta!"

"Huh!" said Oberon. "I've seen the way you look at Theseus! You'd swap me for him in an instant."

"This argument is all your fault, Oberon." Titania accused. "And our fighting is bad for the forest. There's flooding and fog, the flowers can't grow and even the moon isn't as bright as it should be."

"So give me the boy," said Oberon, "and I'll forgive you."

"Forgive me!?" Titania shouted. "Oh, this is ridiculous! Come on, fairies," she called, "we don't need him. Let's go and find a place to dance and cast our spells."

Oberon was left fuming. "Right," he said. "I'll teach her a lesson."

He turned to his servant Puck. "Puck, remember that magical love-flower I showed you, with little purple petals? Go and fetch some for me now, as fast as you can."

"At once, sir," sang Puck.

Fetch me that flower, the herb I showed thee once –
The juice of it on sleeping eyelids laid
Will make or man or woman madly dote
Upon the next live creature that it sees.

What does that mean!?
"Thee" means you, and "madly dote upon" means "fall madly in love with".

"I'll show Titania," Oberon declared. "I'll squeeze the juice of that flower onto her eyes when she's asleep. Then, when she wakes up, it will make her fall in love instantly with the first thing she sees. Whether it's a bear, a wolf or a monkey! Hee hee hee!" he chortled. "And she'll have to do what I want before I set her free!"

Then Oberon heard human voices, and saw two young Athenians approaching.

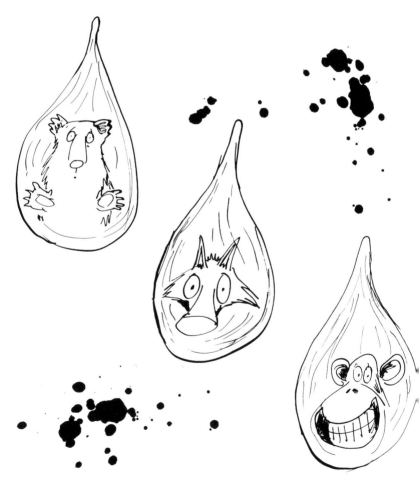

"Helena," the man said. "It was nice of you to tell me about Hermia and Lysander's plan, but could you go away now? I'm sure I can find them myself."

"Let me come too," Helena panted, trying to keep up. "We'll keep each other company."

"Look, Helena," Demetrius snapped. "I've been totally honest with you. I'm sorry, but I don't love you any more."

"But I love you," Helena pleaded.

"Oh, for goodness sake, leave me alone!" Demetrius shouted, and he stormed off into the trees. Helena ran after him.

Oberon watched them go. "Oh dear, oh dear," he said. "What a shame. I'm sure I can do something to help that poor, lovesick girl."

Just then, Puck came back with the sweet-scented, purple flowers.

"Ah, Puck, thank you," said Oberon. "I'll take some of these and go and find Titania."

Then he handed some flowers back to Puck. "You take the rest – I have a little job for you. I've just seen two young people from Athens in the forest – a young man, and a lady who's hopelessly in love with him. But he doesn't love her back, the poor thing. When they're sleeping, put the flower juice on his eyes – so that when he wakes up and sees her, he'll fall in love with her, and then they'll both be happy. You'll find them – they're wearing Athenian clothes."

"Certainly, my lord," said Puck.

On a soft, mossy riverbank covered with violets, wood-roses and thyme flowers, Titania danced and sang with her fairy servants. Then, telling them to watch out for snakes and spiders while she slept, she lay down on a bed of soft thistledown and was soon snoring peacefully.

Oberon sneaked up and quickly squeezed a little flower juice onto her eyes. Just a moment later, he was gone.

I know a bank where the wild thyme blows,
Where oxlips and the nodding violet grows,
Quite overcanopied with luscious woodbine,
With sweet musk-roses and with eglantine.
There sleeps Titania...

What does that mean!?
Oberon describes the beautiful riverbank setting, and all the different flowers that grow on the ground or "over canopy" - hang above the bank from the trees.

When Lysander and Hermia came along, weary from walking through the forest, they saw nothing magical – just the soft, inviting bank of moss and flowers.

"I'm so sorry, my love," Lysander sighed. "I think we've lost our way, and it's getting so late. Let's sleep here, and in the morning, it will be much easier to find the road to my aunt's house."

Hermia nodded. "I could sleep anywhere, I'm so tired," she yawned. "This riverbank looks perfect." So they curled up together on the moss and soon fell fast asleep.

Not long after that, Puck darted into the clearing. "Ah, here they are!" he cried. "I've been looking everywhere. This must be them – a young man and a lady, wearing Athenian clothes. And they're already asleep!"

He flew closer, holding his love-flowers. "What a beautiful girl!" he exclaimed. "How can the man not love her? What a fool!" he said, squeezing plenty of juice onto Lysander's eyes. "Take that. Now you'll love her even more than she loves you."

As soon as he had gone, Helena also arrived at the riverbank. She had followed Demetrius for hours, but she couldn't keep up. Now she was all alone in the forest at night, shivering and frightened.

Then, to her amazement, she saw Lysander and Hermia lying asleep on the ground. "Thank goodness!" she cried. She shook Lysander awake. "Lysander, it's me, Helena! I'm lost in the forest! Demetrius has left me all alone!"

Lysander stared at her. Then he sat bolt upright and declared, "Helena, my beloved! What a beautiful sight to wake up to! Let me kiss you!"

"What!?" said Helena. "Wake up, Lysander – it's me, Helena. I'm not your girlfriend. Look – Hermia's right there. She's the one you love."

"I know you're Helena," said Lysander, "and I love you. Forget Hermia. She's an ugly raven compared to you, my beautiful dove!"

"You're teasing me!" cried Helena. "It's all a joke to you, isn't it, that I'm so unlucky in love? Well, it's not funny. Get away from me."

She stormed off into the trees, but Lysander got up and ran after her. "I'll follow you forever, my darling!" he called.

Hermia rolled over to cuddle up closer to Lysander, and woke up with a start to find herself alone.

"Lysander!?" she wailed. "Lysander, where are you!?" Fearing that he might have been dragged away by a bear or a wolf, poor Hermia got up and ran off into the forest to look for him.

Chapter Three

Apart from the sleeping fairy queen, the flowery riverbank was empty once more. So when Quince and his friends found it, they decided it was the perfect place to rehearse their play.

"It's a bit late," said Quince, "but the moonlight is bright. Look, we can use this bush as a backstage area. Is everyone ready to start? Bottom and Flute, you're on first, as the lovers, Pyramus and Thisbe."

I'm not sure about this

"Erm, Quince..." Bottom began. "I've been reading the play, and I think it's too scary. Pyramus kills himself with a sword, and what about the lion? The ladies in the audience will be terrified!"

"Hmm, you're right," said Quince. "I know – let's add a prologue at the start of the play. We'll explain that it's not real, we're just actors, and the daggers and blood are fake. And Snug can show them that the lion is just a costume. Right, let's get started."

"But Quince," said Bottom, "in the first scene, Pyramus and Thisbe talk to each other through a hole in a wall. We'll never get a wall onto the stage. What are we going to do?"

"Oh dear," said Quince. "I hadn't thought of that."

God shield us! – a lion among ladies is a most dreadful thing. For there is not a more fearful wildfowl than your lion living.

What does that mean!?
Bottom worries about the lion, saying "God shield us", meaning protect us. He calls the lion a "wildfowl" or bird, revealing that he's a bit confused about what a lion is.

"I know," said Bottom. "Someone will have to wear a wall costume, and play the wall. Snout, you can do it, as you're not in this scene. Make a gap between your fingers, to act as the hole."

So Snout stood between Bottom and Flute, and held his hand out with his fingers apart.

At that moment, Puck arrived at the riverbank, though no one saw him. "What on earth is going on here!?" he exclaimed, and stayed to watch.

Playing the part of Pyramus, Bottom crouched down to speak to Flute through the wall.

"Oh, Thisbe mine," he declared loudly. "Your breath smells... Erm, what's next, Quince? I've forgotten!"

"It's 'Your breath smells like sweet flowers!' " said Quince. "Not 'Your breath smells'!"

"Oh yes, sorry," said Bottom. "Your breath smells like sweet flowers!"

"Oh, Pyramus, my love!" squeaked Flute, putting on his girliest voice. "I could talk to you for hours!"

"Lovely," said Quince. "You're next, Bottom."

"Oh yes," said Bottom. "Hark, what's that noise? I'll go and see. Sweet Thisbe, stay and wait for me!"

"Now go behind the bush!" hissed Quince.

"What?"

"Offstage, behind the bush!" Quince yelled.

Oh, Thisbe mine!

33

"Goodness me," said Puck. "This is absolute rubbish. I'll liven things up a bit." So he cast a quick spell to turn Bottom's head into a donkey's.

"Bottom, come back, you're on again!" called Quince. Bottom stumbled out from behind the bush, shouting, "Thisbe, 'tis I, your darling man. Come and **kiss** me if you can!"

Oh, monstrous! Oh, strange! We are haunted. Pray, masters! Fly, masters! Help!

What does that mean!?
Quince yells at his friends ("masters") to "fly", or run away.

AAAAARRRGGGGHH!" screamed Quince when he saw the hideous creature. "It's a monster of the forest!" he wailed. "An evil spirit! Run, everyone!" The workmen all backed away in terror, then turned and ran for home as fast as they could.

"Where have they all gone?" Bottom wondered. "What's going on!?"

Just then, Titania stirred, stretched and yawned. She opened her eyes, and the very first thing she saw was Bottom.

"What angel is this?" she gasped. "Why, you are more beautiful than any man I have ever seen!"

"Really?" said Bottom, puzzled. "Who are you?"

"I am the fairy queen, my darling, and I want to keep you by my side forever! I love you!"

"But I have to go back to Athens and find my friends!" Bottom protested. "We're putting on a play."

"Never mind that, my handsome one," Titania soothed. "Come with me, and my fairies will feed you sweet nectar, and fan you with their fairy wings."

"Erm... OK," said Bottom, and he allowed Titania to lead him away.

"So, Puck," Oberon asked, "Is your work done?"

"Yes sir, and more besides!" sang Puck with glee. "I put the flower juice on the young man's eyes. I also met another poor idiot from Athens, Bottom the weaver, and gave him a donkey's head. And guess what – he was the first thing Titania saw when she woke up, so she's in love with him!"

What **angel** wakes me from my flowery bed?

"Brilliant!" Oberon chuckled. "It's worked a treat!"

Then they saw Demetrius coming through the forest, followed this time by Hermia.

"Here's the young man," said Oberon, "but who's that lady? She wasn't the one I saw."

"I've never seen him before," said Puck. "It was another man I found, with this lady beside him."

"Demetrius, come back!" Hermia called. "What are you doing in the forest, and where is Lysander? Demetrius, what have you done? Did you follow us, and kill Lysander so you could marry me?"

"Hermia! Of course not!" said Demetrius. "I don't care about him. I came to find you, and stop you."

"Typical!" fumed Hermia. "Well, I'd never marry you, even if Lysander was dead!"

She ran away, and Demetrius sat down gloomily. "This is a disaster," he moaned, "and I'm worn out. I think I'll just try to get some sleep on this nice soft riverbank."

He lay down and
closed his eyes.

"Oh dear, Puck," said Oberon.
"I think you got the wrong man.
This is the man I meant. We need to
put this right. Quick – go and find the other
girl." While Puck was gone, Oberon put some
flower juice on Demetrius's eyes.

39

In a flash, Puck was back with Helena and Lysander. "I've found her, sir," he said, "but this man is in love with her now! Look!"

"Helena, be mine, I beg you!" Lysander pleaded. "I love you more than words can say!"

"Lysander, stop winding me up and go back to Hermia!" Helena said. "Oh look!" she gasped. "Here's Demetrius!"

Her voice woke Demetrius up, and he opened his eyes. He gazed at Helena.

"Helena!" he whispered. "Where have you been!? I've missed you so much, my love!"

"What? What's going on!?" demanded Helena.

"I love you, Helena!" Demetrius declared, kneeling before her.

"No!" shouted Lysander, shoving him out of the way. "I love Helena."

"No, you don't!" Demetrius said. "You love Hermia!"

"You can have Hermia," shrugged Lysander. "Look, here she comes!"

"Lysander! There you are!" Hermia called.

"Go away, Hermia," said Lysander. "I love Helena now." Hermia stared at him in confusion.

"Stop it, stop it, all of you!" Helena begged, now with tears in her eyes. "You're all just playing a trick on me. I know no one loves me. This is too cruel. Hermia, I thought you were my friend."

41

"I am," said Hermia. "Lysander, Demetrius,
why are you doing this?"

"Because I love Helena!" said Lysander. "And if Demetrius
loves her too, I'll challenge him to a duel. The winner can
marry Helena!"

"You're on!" said Demetrius, and they went off to find
a place to fight.

"Don't be ridiculous!" said Helena, running after them,
with Hermia following close behind.

"Oops!" said Puck.

"Puck, you've messed this up completely!" scolded Oberon.
"Go after them, and cast a thick fog over them, so they can't
see each other to fight. Then make a spell to send them
to sleep. It's almost dawn – we have to work fast."

Oberon reached down and plucked a different,
lily-white flower from the riverbank.

"This flower can undo the magic. Squeeze it into
Lysander's eyes. Then he'll go back to being in love
with Hermia, and we should end up with two happy
couples.

"And meanwhile," added the fairy king with a smirk,
"I'll go and see how Titania's getting on!"

Chapter Four

Oberon found Titania under a tree, with Bottom lying beside her, his enormous head in her lap.

"Let me stroke your cheeks, and kiss your lovely big ears," she cooed. Oberon tried not to giggle.

Titania's fairy servants waited on Bottom's every wish, feeding him honey and berries, playing him fairy music, and even scratching his head for him.

'What else can we bring you, my beloved darling?" asked Titania.

'It's strange, but I really fancy a handful of oats,' said Bottom. "Or maybe some hay? But don't worry – what I really want is a nice snooze."

'We'll both sleep,' said Titania. She sent her fairies away, and lay down with Bottom, her arms entwined around his hairy neck. "Oh, how I love you!" she sighed, before dropping off.

'Puck!' whispered Oberon. "Come and see this! It's hilarious!" Puck appeared by his side, sniggering at the ridiculous sight.

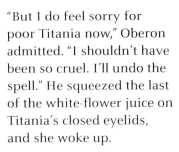

"But I do feel sorry for poor Titania now," Oberon admitted. "I shouldn't have been so cruel. I'll undo the spell." He squeezed the last of the white-flower juice on Titania's closed eyelids, and she woke up.

"Oberon...? I've just had the craziest dream," said Titania. "I thought I was in love with a donkey!"

"What, that one right there?" said Oberon, pointing to the snoring Bottom.

"Oh, Oberon!" Titania gasped. "What was I thinking!?"

"It was my fault," Oberon confessed, "and I'm sorry. Let's be friends and put everything back to normal. It's almost time for the duke's wedding."

He turned to Puck. "Puck, turn poor Bottom back into himself. When he wakes up, along with those two young couples, they'll all think it's just been a strange midsummer night's dream."

What does that mean!?
"Methought" means I thought, "enamoured of" means in love with, and "ass" is another word for a donkey.

The sound of dogs barking echoed through the trees, and Duke Theseus, his bride-to-be Hippolyta, and Hermia's father Egeus appeared.

It was May Day, and Egeus, desperate to find his daughter, had asked Theseus for help. They all set out with their hunting dogs to search for her. And, with a little invisible help from the fairies, they soon arrived at the right spot.

"Look, here they are, on the ground!" said Theseus. "All four of them, safe and sound and fast asleep!"

"Thank goodness Hermia's safe!" Egeus cried. He shook them all awake in turn. "What are you all doing here together?"

Lysander stretched and yawned, then looked puzzled. "Truly, sir, I don't know how we reached this spot. Hermia and I ran away to get married..."

48

"I knew it!" Egeus said to Hermia. "You planned to disobey me, and marry Lysander instead of Demetrius!"

"But I don't mind," said Demetrius mildly. "None of that matters any more. It all seems like a dream. In fact, I still feel like I'm dreaming. I've realised who I really love – Helena." He took her hand, and Lysander took Hermia's.

"But... but..." Egeus spluttered.

Theseus turned to him. "Egeus, can't you see these young people are in love? I've had enough of silly rules, and I'm overriding your wishes. They shall all be married today, alongside me and Hippolyta."

"Today?" said Hermia.

Are you sure
That we are awake? It seems to me
That yet we sleep, we dream.

"Three nights have gone by since you disappeared," Theseus said. "It's May Day, my wedding day. If you agree to a joint wedding, come to the temple at noon."

What does that mean!?

Demetrius wonders if he has really woken up, as it seems to him that they could all still ("yet") be dreaming.

49

Meanwhile, Bottom also woke up, blinking in the sunshine. "Where is everyone?" he said. "That was the weirdest dream ever! But I must get back to Athens!" He jumped to his feet and ran off.

Bottom's friends were all at Quince's house, looking worried.

"It's May Day morning!" Quince fretted.
"If Bottom doesn't turn up soon,
we can't do our play!"

"I'm here!"

"He's not at his house," said Snug. "We've checked."

"No one can play Pyramus but Bottom," Quince moaned. "He's the best! I just hope he's OK."

Just then, Bottom rushed in. "I'm here, everyone, I'm here!"

"Bottom!" they all cried. "Where have you been!?"

"You won't believe the strange things that happened to me in the forest!" said Bottom. "But there's no time to tell you now! The wedding has already started! Come on, we've got to go!"

Chapter Five

They all grabbed their props and costumes, tumbled out of the door and headed for the palace.

And so, back in Athens, Theseus and
Hippolyta, Hermia and Lysander,
and Demetrius and Helena were
all married at the temple.
During the wedding feast,
Theseus sent for Philostrate.
"It's time to choose the
entertainments," he
said. "What do you
have lined up?"
Theseus asked.

"It's all here, sir!" said Philostrate, producing a list.

"Now, let me see," Theseus said. "Harp music... hmm. The story of Hercules... no, heard it before. Ah – *The Most Lamentable Comedy and Most Cruel Death of Pyramus and Thisbe*. What's this?"

"Ah, yes, sir. From what I've seen, it's a bunch of half-witted workmen who really can't act, and the play is dire! It's supposed to be a tragedy, and it did bring tears to my eyes, sir, but tears of laughter!"

"That sounds perfect!" said Theseus. "We'll have the play!"

The workmen were thrilled when Philostrate called them into the great hall. As they set up their props, Quince delivered the prologue he had written:

I will hear that play. For never anything can be amiss When simpleness and duty tender it. Go, bring them in.

What does that mean!?
Theseus chooses the play, saying nothing can go wrong ("amiss") if it's done with honesty, or "simpleness".

Ladies and gentlemen, please enjoy
Our woeful tale of girl meets boy.
We don't want to ruin the surprise,
But at the end, everyone dies.
But never fear! It's just a show,
No one will really die, you know!
The blood is fake, kept in this cup,
And the lion is just our Snug, dressed up!

"Bravo!" shouted Theseus, and everyone laughed and clapped. Then the show began. Bottom and Flute came onto the stage, along with Snout, dressed up as the Wall.

I am Thisbe's garden Wall,
said Snout.
And in me, there's
a little hole!
Here, the two lovers
meet by night
And talk through the hole
in the bright moonlight!

Oh, Thisbe mine, your breath smells like sweet flowers! Bottom shouted through the wall.

Oh, Pyramus! I could talk
to you for hours!
squeaked Flute.

Hark, what's that noise?
I'll go and see, said Bottom.
Sweet Thisbe, stay and wait for me!

"This is absolutely brilliant," Theseus laughed.
"A talking wall! What do you think, Demetrius?"

"It's the cleverest talking wall I've ever seen, my lord!"
Demetrius smiled. "Oh look, Pyramus is coming back!"
Bottom ran back onto the stage.

Thisbe, 'tis I, your darling man.
Come and kiss me if you can!
Thisbe, where have you gone, my dear?

It's too dark to see me, but I'm right here!
said Flute.

Kiss me then, darling, through
the wall! said Bottom.

Bottom and Flute stuck their lips out and tried to reach each other through the wall, but it was too thick. Theseus was rolling about with laughter.

I'm just kissing the wall, not your lips at all! Flute said. *Let's meet in the graveyard instead! We'll be safe there, as everyone is dead.*

By now, the whole audience was laughing out loud, and cheered the Wall loudly as he went off.

"Shhhh!" said Quince. "Now it's the graveyard scene." Flute, as Thisbe, came on alone.

Pyramus, where are you? Pyramus, my dear? But what's that roaring noise I hear?

Rooooooaaaaaarrr! roared Snug, leaping onstage in his lion costume. "Don't worry, ladies," he added, peeping out for a moment from behind his mask. "It's just me, Snug the joiner!" *Roooooaaar!*

The lion chased Flute around until it caught him by cloak.
Then Flute ran off, and the lion tore the cloak to shreds. Finally,
the lion took a bow, to a round of applause, and left the stage,
as Bottom ran back on.

*Sorry I'm late! What was that
roaring sound!?*
*Look, here's Thisbe's cloak on
the ground!*
Alas, a lion's eaten her up!
And so I will die too!
Where's that cup?

Quince quickly passed Bottom
the cup, and he pretended to stab
himself, splashing the fake blood
everywhere.

"This is the silliest thing I've ever
seen!" said Hippolyta.
"I agree, they are truly dreadful,"
said Theseus. "But everyone's
having a great time! We couldn't
have asked for more fun at our
wedding feast!"

Flute ran back on stage as Thisbe,
to find Bottom lying on the ground.

Pyramus! Pyramus! Oh no!
He's dead! Oh woe is me, oh woe!
Oh, Pyramus! I loved him so.
He had such nice green eyes,
  you know.
And lovely lips and nostrils too.
And so, I know what I must do.
I cannot live, so I must die!
Now, where's that knife? Goodbye,
  goodbye!

The iron tongue of midnight
hath told twelve.
Lovers, to bed. 'Tis almost fairy time.

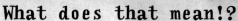

What does that mean!?
Theseus describes the bell ringing
at midnight as an "iron tongue".
The word "'Tis" is short for "It is".

Flute grabbed the dagger from Bottom's hand and pretended to stab himself too, collapsing onto the stage. The crowd went wild, cheering and clapping, and all the actors came back on to take a bow.

"Thank you, my friends, for a most excellent entertainment," said Theseus. "The hour is late, and we must all go to bed – for it's after midnight, and that, as we know, is the fairies' time."

Everyone made their way home to bed. Then, above the palace, Oberon and Titania danced and flew and sprinkled magic spells, so that Theseus and Hippolyta, Hermia and Lysander, and Helena and Demetrius would live happily ever after.

61

A MIDSUMMER NIGHT'S DREAM AT A GLANCE

A Midsummer Night's Dream is Shakespeare at his most humorous. It uses basic comedy devices, like mistaken identity and slapstick silliness. As magic is involved, all the problems are easily solved, and like most comedies from Shakespeare's era, the play ends with a wedding.

A Midsummer Night's Dream as a play

Although this book tells the story in prose, *A Midsummer Night's Dream* is really a play, written to be performed on the stage. The play takes the form of dialogue, or words spoken by the characters – there are no other descriptions or explanations, apart from the stage directions (instructions for the actors, which are not read out).

This is the opening of a scene from *A Midsummer Night's Dream*, as Shakespeare wrote it:

ACT 3

Scene 2. [Another part of the wood] *Stage directions*

Enter OBERON, King of fairies, solus*. *alone

OBERON: Then, what it was that next came in her eye,
Which she must dote on in extremity*. *adore completely

[Enter PUCK]
Here comes my messenger.
How now, mad spirit!
What night-rule* now about this haunted grove? *chaos

FACT FILE:
FULL TITLE: A Midsummer Night's Dream
DATE WRITTEN: around 1594
LENGTH: 2,186 lines – quite short for a Shakespeare play

Acts and scenes

Shakespeare's plays have five main sections, or acts, split into
smaller sections called scenes, each set in a different place.
This breaks down the play into chunks, helping Shakespeare
to set up the play's events, and the actors to learn their parts.

THE FIVE ACTS OF *A MIDSUMMER NIGHT'S DREAM*

ACT 1 (2 scenes)
Hermia and Lysander and the
workmen all plan to meet in the forest.

ACT 2 (2 scenes)
Oberon's love potion starts
to cause problems when Puck
uses it on the wrong man.

ACT 3 (2 scenes)
While Bottom gets a donkey's head and
Titania falls in love with him, Puck rescues
the young lovers from their mix-up.

ACT 4 (2 scenes)
Everything is sorted out and
Bottom gets home just in
time to perform the play.

ACT 5 (1 scene)
The wedding takes place, with the
workmen's play as entertainment.

THE STORY OF
A MIDSUMMER NIGHT'S DREAM

Shakespeare usually borrowed the stories for his plays from history, legends or folktales. *A Midsummer Night's Dream* is an exception, as Shakespeare seems to have made up most of the storyline himself. However, many of the play's characters do come from old stories and myths.

Theseus and Hippolyta

Theseus is an important figure in ancient Greek mythology. According to legend, he was half god and half human, and did marry Hippolyta, queen of the Amazons, as he does in the play. Shakespeare probably read about Theseus in the works of two great Roman writers, Plutarch and Ovid.

Theseus also features in the works of Geoffrey Chaucer, an important English writer who lived in the 1300s, 200 years before Shakespeare. So he would have been a well-known character for Shakespeare's audiences.

Geoffrey
Chaucer

Pyramus and Thisbe

The workmen's play is the tale of star-crossed lovers Pyramus and Thisbe. The Roman writer Ovid included the story in his most famous work, *Metamorphoses*. There are also some similarities between *Pyramus and Thisbe* and Shakespeare's tragedy *Romeo and Juliet*, which he wrote at around the same time as *A Midsummer Night's Dream*.

64

Sprites and fairies

Oberon, the fairy king, first appeared in
medieval poems and songs, and was based on a dwarf
or wizard from German legend. Puck, or Robin Goodfellow,
was a magical sprite or goblin from English folklore.
However, Shakespeare made up Titania and the other fairies,
as well as the workmen and the four young human lovers.

Athens

The play is set in ancient
Greece in the real city of
Athens. Today, it's Greece's
capital, and in ancient times
it was the centre of the Greek
world. It was surrounded by a
city wall, with forests growing
outside it.

SHAKESPEARE AND
A MIDSUMMER NIGHT'S DREAM

Today, we think of Shakespeare's work as great art. But for Shakespeare, being a playwright wasn't just a way of being creative. It was a busy, demanding job. Shakespeare had to keep writing plays to a high standard to meet the needs of the successful theatre company he worked for.

Shakespeare the showman

Sometime around 1590, Shakespeare moved to London from his hometown of Stratford-upon-Avon. He probably began his career as an actor. In 1594, around the time he wrote *A Midsummer Night's Dream*, he became a member and part-owner of a new theatre company, the Chamberlain's Men. He was to spend many years with them as an actor, playwright and manager.

Even better than his last one!

Writing for success

The company needed new plays all the time, to keep pulling in the paying crowds. Shakespeare was their star writer, producing popular plays in many different styles – comedies, tragedies and history plays. He was a bit like TV scriptwriters today, who write shows such as *Dr Who*.

Written for a wedding?

No one knows what prompted Shakespeare to write *A Midsummer Night's Dream* – it could have just been one of the many comic plays he wrote for the stage. But some experts think he might have written it specially to be performed at a celebrity wedding – possibly the wedding of Elizabeth Carey and Thomas Berkeley in 1595.

Elizabeth Carey was a society lady, dancer, writer and courtier. The poets of the 1590s often dedicated their works to her. If Shakespeare did write the play for her or for another wedding, then the plot itself echoes this with its own play – the one the workmen perform at Theseus's wedding. Shakespeare often used echoes like this in his works.

STAGING A MIDSUMMER NIGHT'S DREAM

When *A Midsummer Night's Dream* was written, the Chamberlain's Men used a theatre called "The Theatre". Later, they built another theatre, the Globe. *A Midsummer Night's Dream* was probably performed at both of them.

The Theatre

The Theatre was one of the first proper theatres in London. James Burbage, the founder of Shakespeare's company the Chamberlain's men, had built it in 1576. Before this, plays were usually put on in large houses or inn courtyards, not purpose-built theatres.

Theatres in Shakespeare's time were round and open-air.

Theatre stars

Several of the star actors of Shakespeare's time were members of the Chamberlain's Men. They included Richard Burbage (James's son), who usually played lead roles, and Will Kempe, a famous clown. We don't know for sure, but Kempe is very likely to have played the part of Bottom. Shakespeare may even have written it specially for him.

Seeing a show

Theatres in Shakespeare's time weren't quiet, polite places. They were more like today's cinemas – people chatted, ate snacks and wandered to and fro during the show. As most theatres were open-air, plays were shown in the afternoon, while it was still light. All the actors were male, so boys with higher voices usually played the female parts.

As companies put on several plays a week, it was hard to set up lots of scenery. Instead, the actors' costumes and the language of the play had to set the scene – like when Oberon describes the flowery glade:

I know a bank where the wild thyme blows, where oxlips and the nodding violet grows . . .

Flying fairies

Theatres in Shakespeare's time had a ceiling over the stage, and actors could dangle through a trap door in the ceiling on ropes, to look as if they were flying. It's possible this was used in *A Midsummer Night's Dream*.

Fun Fact!

A Midsummer Night's Dream is a popular play for outdoor performances today. It's often performed in summer in Regent's Park in London.

A MIDSUMMER NIGHT'S DREAM: THEMES AND SYMBOLS

Many of Shakespeare's plays contain repeated themes and symbols – ideas and images that run all the way through. They help to hold the play together, to reinforce what it's about, and to emphasize particular characters.

Here are some of the main themes and symbols in *A Midsummer Night's Dream*:

Chaos and order

The characters in *A Midsummer Night's Dream* constantly try to unpick tangled problems and create order out of chaos.

• Theseus wants to fix the row between Hermia and her father, so she can marry who she wants.

• Oberon wants to help the young lovers pair up, but makes things even worse.

• The workmen struggle with many aspects of their play and have to keep changing it.

• As the play is a comedy, everything is eventually neatly sorted out, leading to a happy ending.

Sleep and dreams

The action takes place at night, and there are at least 10 instances of people going to sleep! Sleep is a time when magical changes can take place, moving the story forward – Oberon's love potion, for example, works on people's eyes while they sleep.

There aren't any real dreams in the play – instead, people think they must have been dreaming to explain their strange, magical experiences. Yet while they sleep, three nights magically pass in what seems like one.

HERMIA:
Be it so, Lysander.
Find you out a bed,
for I upon this bank
will rest my head.

TITANIA:
Sing me
now asleep.

FAIRIES:
Lulla, lulla, lullaby,
Lulla, lulla, lullaby...

Women and men

In the play, Shakespeare deals with an important issue – a struggle for power between men and women. Egeus thinks Hermia must obey him because he's her father, and Athenian law backs him up. Oberon thinks Titania must obey him because he's her husband. These ideas reflect what life was really like for women in Shakespeare's time. Yet the female characters resist strongly, and their disagreement underlies almost everything that happens in the play.

FAIRIES!

A Midsummer Night's Dream is famous for its fairies. They always make a beautiful spectacle on the stage, and costume and set designers over the years have created amazing outfits and special effects for Titania, Oberon, and all their fairy servants. But what did they mean to Shakespeare and his audiences?

Fairy folklore

In Elizabethan times, many people really believed in fairies. They were thought to be supernatural beings that looked like smallish humans – though, of course, they were usually invisible.

According to legend, fairies loved bread, milk and cream and would reward people who left food out for them – for example, by cleaning and tidying their house overnight. However, they could also punish people they didn't like, by doing things such as pinching them as they slept. Fairies were also said to steal babies and carry them away to fairyland, replacing them with a "changeling" – a fairy or goblin baby.

Goblin baby

Shakespeare's fairies

In *A Midsummer Night's Dream*, Shakespeare developed fairies into something more powerfully magical, yet also less solid – able to disappear, pass unharmed through a flame, or zoom around the world in seconds. The play describes them as if they are tiny (even though it's not possible for them appear that way on stage). Titania orders her fairies to make little coats from bats' wings, and Oberon says they can wrap themselves in old, shed snakeskins.

Over park, over pale*,
Through flood, through fire,
I do wander everywhere,
Swifter than the moon's sphere.

*enclosed field

Fairy characters

Shakespeare also gives his fairies very human, realistic personalities. They quarrel, tease each other and show love and kindness too.

These Shakespeare-style fairies have influenced writers ever since. They helped to create our modern idea of a fairy – a tiny, translucent, flying creature. Although Shakespeare himself didn't show fairies with wings, they almost always have them in modern productions of the play.

73

THE LANGUAGE OF
A *MIDSUMMER NIGHT'S DREAM*

For writing his plays, Shakespeare mainly used a type of poetry called blank verse. Blank verse has five "beats" per line, and doesn't usually rhyme. Within his lines of verse, Shakespeare used poetic methods such as metaphors and alliteration to conjure up beautiful images, or emphasize the characters' feelings at emotional moments.

*** Sometimes one character starts a line of blank verse, and another finishes it.

Repetition: repeating a word or phrase creates an echoing rhythm to reinforce an idea.

Hippolyta: FOUR DAYS WILL QUICKLY steep themselves in night.

FOUR NIGHTS WILL QUICKLY dream away the time.

And then the moon, like to a silver bow**

New bent in heaven, shall behold the night

Of our solemnities.***

Theseus: Go, Philostrate,***

Stir up the Athenian youth to merriments.

Awake the pert and nimble spirit of mirth.*

Turn melancholy* forth to funerals.

** Simile: something is described as being like something else – the new moon is like a silver bow (as in a bow and arrow) because of its curved shape.

Metaphors: something is described as being or doing something else, as a way of comparing them. Hippolyta says the moon "shall behold the night of our solemnities", meaning watch the wedding, as a way to describe it rising on that night.

* Alliteration: pairs or patterns of words with the same first letter. This is used to make melancholy (sadness) and mirth (laughter) into a pair in order to draw a contrast between them.

Everyday speech

Sometimes, Shakespeare's characters speak in prose, or normal speech. In *A Midsummer Night's Dream*, the workmen mainly use prose. It's often used in comedy scenes, or for servants and workmen, to reflect the normal, everyday atmosphere of working life.

BOTTOM: Let me play the lion too. I will roar, that I will do any man's heart good to hear me. I will roar, that I will make the duke say, "Let him roar again. Let him roar again."

Did you know?

Shakespeare sometimes made up new words when he couldn't find one that would do. The words "flowery", "moonbeam" and "fancy-free", which we still use today, first appear in *A Midsummer Night's Dream*.

WHAT *A MIDSUMMER NIGHT'S DREAM* MEANS NOW

Shakespeare is still loved, read and performed
because his timeless themes, ideas and messages still
have meaning for us today. As a romantic comedy,
A Midsummer Night's Dream still works just as it would
have done when it was first shown, over 400 years ago.
Today, as well as being performed often, the play has also
been made into ballets, operas and films.

Love and unrequited love

Love stories have existed ever since writing began.
Most people feel drawn to the idea of falling in
love. So there are countless tales of love that
goes wrong, is unrequited (not returned), or
has to overcome obstacles – with a happy
ending when the problems are solved.
You can find the same pattern in countless
romcom films and "chick-lit" novels.

Comedy confusion

While jokes relating to the politics or
fashions of 400 years ago would not be
funny now, the mix-ups and mistakes
in *A Midsummer Night's Dream* still
make us laugh. Watch any TV sitcom
and you'll see the same methods used –
mistaken identity, misunderstandings,
and people being hilariously bad at
things, like the workmen and their play.

Slapstick

Shakespeare also uses visual comedy – things that are funny to look at, like Bottom with a donkey's head, or Snout dressed up as a wall. The simpler the joke, the better it translates through time. If you watch a production or film of *A Midsummer Night's Dream* today, you'll see that these things are still used to get the biggest laughs!

Fantasy, magic and spells

In Shakespeare's time, people were fascinated by the world of fairies, elves and witches, and the possibility of magic. And, despite centuries of advancing technology, we still are today. Popular books, films and TV shows are still full of fantasy themes like wizards, vampires and magical abilities. It seems to be part of human nature to be fascinated by supernatural forces.

GLOSSARY

alliteration	Grouping together words with the same initial letter
bellows	Device for blowing air at a fire
blank verse	Type of non-rhyming poetry used by Shakespeare
dramatis personae	List of characters in a play
folklore	Traditional tales, legends and beliefs
lamentable	Sad
metaphor	Describing something by saying it is another thing
prologue	An introduction at the start of a story or play, given by a narrator
prose	Text written in ordinary sentences, not in verse
romcom	Short for romantic comedy
simile	Describing something by saying it is like something else
slapstick	Clownish, physical humour, such as people falling over or bumping into each other
stage directions	Instructions for the actors in a play
supernatural	Magical or beyond the laws of nature
symbol	Something that stands for an idea or object
tinker	Someone who mends household utensils and tools
translucent	Letting light through
woo	To pursue someone as a romantic partner

GLOSSARY OF SHAKESPEARE'S LANGUAGE

bent	determined
dote (on)	to adore or admire someone
doth	does
faith	really, indeed, or I swear!
fly	run away
methought	I thought
mirth	fun and laughter
o'er	over
pale	an enclosed area or field for keeping animals in
pert	cheeky or high-spirited
solus	alone
thee	you

A MIDSUMMER NIGHT'S DREAM QUIZ

Test yourself and your friends on the story, characters and language of Shakespeare's *A Midsummer Night's Dream*. You can find the answers at the bottom of the page.

1) At the start of the play, both Demetrius and Lysander want to marry Hermia – but who does she end up with?
2) What is Theseus's servant called?
3) Who does Lysander think can help him marry Hermia?
4) Name two of the workmen's jobs.
5) What do Oberon and Titania fight over?
6) Who plays the Wall in the workmen's play?
7) Name three of the plants Oberon describes growing in the forest.
8) What does Bottom feel like eating when he has a donkey's head?
9) Who does Theseus discuss the Wall's performance with?
10) Who visits Theseus's palace after the wedding party?

10) *Oberon and Titania*
9) *Demetrius*
8) *Oats and hay*
7) *Thyme, oxlip, violet, woodbine, musk, rose, eglantine*
6) *Snout*
5) *A little human boy*
4) *Carpenter, weaver, joiner, tinker, tailor, bellows-maker*
3) *His aunt*
2) *Philostrate*
1) *Lysander*

MACBETH

978 0 7502 9109 5

HAMLET

978 0 7502 9113 2

A MIDSUMMER NIGHT'S DREAM

978 0 7502 9110 1

THE TEMPEST

978 0 7502 9115 6

ROMEO AND JULIET

978 0 7502 9111 8

MUCH ADO ABOUT NOTHING

978 0 7502 9114 9